*Joy to the World* copyright © Frances Lincoln Limited 1998
Text copyright © Saviour Pirotta 1998
Illustrations copyright © Sheila Moxley 1998

First published in Great Britain in 1998 by
Frances Lincoln Limited, 4 Torriano Mews
Torriano Avenue, London NW5 2RZ

British Library Cataloguing in Publication Data
available on request

ISBN 0-7112-1254-6

Set in Adminster

Printed in Hong Kong

9 8 7 6 5 4 3 2 1

# JOY TO THE WORLD!

## CHRISTMAS STORIES FROM AROUND THE GLOBE

Saviour Pirotta

*Illustrated by* Sheila Moxley

**FRANCES LINCOLN**

*For* FRANCISCO RICARDO JIMENEZ (1961-1995),
teacher, friend and an inspiration to all who
knew him. His memory will long be cherished
by his family in Argentina and by his many
friends around the world ★ S.P

*For* SUE, MAT AND MOLLY ★ S.M

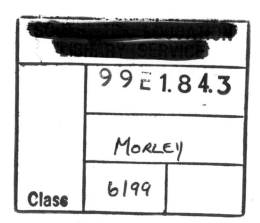

# Contents

# The Brave Little Camel

## A STORY FROM SYRIA

IT WAS a hot day in the middle of summer. A herd of camels was sitting in the shade, munching dried grass and dates.

A wobbly little camel tottered up to his mother.

"Look, Mama," he shouted. "I can run!"

"So you can," said his mother.

The little camel fell over in the mud and waved his wobbly legs. "Oops," he said.

"Oops," Mama laughed.

Mama's friend sighed. "Children nowadays," she said. "They want to run before they can walk."

Just then, the camel-herd came into the stables followed by a well-dressed official.

"I want to buy fourteen camels," said the official.

The camel-herd showed him his camels.

"I'll take those ten big ones over there," said the official, "and those four strong ones sitting by the gate."

"What about this one?" said the camel-herd, pointing to the naughty little camel, who was trying to jump over a stone.

"I can't take that one," said the official. "He's too wobbly."

"He's only two weeks old," said the camel-herd. "Besides, you're buying his mother."

"I can't take him," said the official firmly. "My three wise masters want to cross the desert as quickly as possible. They are visiting a new King who was born yesterday in Bethlehem. This wobbly little camel will hold everyone up."

"No I won't," said the little camel, but of course the official could not understand a word he was saying.

The camel-herd tied all the official's camels into a neat line.

"I'm coming with you," said the little camel to his mother. "I want to see the newborn King."

"All right," said his mother. "But make sure you don't get caught."

When the official led the camels down the street, the wobbly little camel slid past the camel-herd and tiptoed quietly behind his mother. But the official spotted him right away.

"Go home, little camel," said the official.

The little camel pretended to go away. He hid round a corner and stood very still. When the official was looking the other way, the little camel sneaked back to the train again. This time he walked behind a very big camel and the official didn't spot him.

The Three Wise Men and their servants were waiting for the camels on the edge of the village. They had many more camels with them, loaded with food, clothes and splendid gifts for the newborn King.

The little camel's mother was given some carpets to carry. They were rolled up into huge bundles and secured with rope on her back.

"I want to carry one too," said the little camel.

"Be quiet," said his mother. "Someone might hear you."

But the naughty little camel wouldn't be quiet. "I want to carry a carpet for the newborn King," he wailed.

"All right," his mother said patiently. "But don't blame me if you get caught and sent back to the camel-herd." She rolled the smallest carpet off her hump and let it fall on to the little camel's back.

"There," she said. "Is it heavy?"

"Only a bit," said the little camel.

"Keep to the middle of the train," said his mother. "That way, no one will spot you."

The camel train started its journey across the desert. The little camel wobbled and tottered under his carpet. But he wouldn't give up.

"Hurry up," his mother said. "Or you'll get left behind."

The wobbly little camel hurried as fast as he could. But he couldn't help falling behind. His wobbly legs just wouldn't carry him fast enough. At last he was spotted trailing behind the rest by one of the servants.

"There's a carpet walking behind us," said the servant.

The official whisked the carpet off the little camel. "I told you to go back home," he snarled. "Now go away. Shoo!"

The little camel pretended to go away again. He hid behind a dune and waited until the train was moving once more. Then he crept back to his mother.

"I want to see the newborn King," he cried.

"I know," sighed his mother. "But try to behave yourself this time. And don't stay too close to me. The official might come looking for you."

The little camel tried extremely hard to behave. To keep himself going, he tried thinking about the newborn King. What would he look like? he wondered. Would he have a hump like a baby camel? Would he want to play in the sand?

The little camel was so happy to be going to see the newborn King that he forgot to be quiet, and started to dance. He jumped and pranced until he was tired. Then he fell asleep.

When he woke up again, the train had moved on. The little camel was frightened. He called for his mother.

"Help! Help!" he shouted.

He was about to start crying, when he noticed a trail of camel-prints in the sand.

"That's the way my mama went," he thought.

He followed the trail, stumbling along on his wobbly little legs until he could see the camel train in the distance.

"Mama, Mama!" called the little camel breathlessly. "Wait for me. I'm coming to see the newborn King."

The little camel ran faster and faster. But suddenly a sandstorm blew up. The wobbly little camel knelt on the ground and shut his eyes to keep out the sand. When he opened them again, it was pitch dark. The little camel couldn't see the train any more. He looked for his mama's prints in the sand, but the wind had blown them away.

"I'm lost," wailed the little camel. "And I so wanted to see the newborn King."

Just then, a shooting star lit up the sky and the little camel could see his way. Far ahead of him stood the camel train, on the edge of the desert.

"I'm coming, Mama!" called the wobbly little camel.

He broke into a wobbly little trot, keeping his eyes firmly on the train. The shooting star was hovering above, lighting up the sky with gold and silver sparks.

The excited little camel ran faster and faster. He ran across the sand, past his mother and straight into a stable where the Three Wise Men were kneeling. He was going so fast that he couldn't stop. He skidded right into a little manger where a baby lay.

"Not you again!" cried the official.

"Children nowadays!" huffed the grown-up camels.

"Shocking!" gasped some shepherds near the manger.

But the baby's mother, a beautiful lady with long dark hair, smiled and patted the little camel on the head.

"Have you come to see the newborn King?" she asked.

The wobbly little camel nodded.

"And did you come all the way across the desert with your mama?"

The wobbly little camel nodded again.

"You are so brave to have come all that way," said the beautiful lady. She lifted the newborn King out of the manger so that the little camel could see him properly. The little baby King didn't have a hump, but he was as wobbly as the little camel and he had the kindest, wrinkliest face in the world. The little camel wanted to be his friend for ever.

That is why, even today, the little camel goes from house to house at Christmas, bringing presents from the baby Jesus to all the little children.

# Baby in the Bread

## A EUROPEAN STORY SET IN MALTA

THE old baker woman huffed and puffed. She had two hundred loaves to make before breakfast, and there wasn't enough flour left in the sack to make ten. To make matters worse, her right arm was hurting; she'd banged her elbow against the oven door.

"It's all too much for me," grumbled the baker woman to the bakery cat. She pounded the dough with her enormous fists, grunting with the effort.

The baker woman's younger sister came into the bakery.

"The bread seller at the market wants twenty extra loaves tomorrow," she said. "Can you do them?"

The baker woman shook her head. "I haven't enough flour," she said. "The harvest was terrible."

"How can people expect to survive without bread?" said her sister. "I wish the Romans would do something about it."

"The Romans don't seem to care about us," said the baker woman. "Nobody does."

"It's sad to see people going hungry all the time," said her sister. She wrapped a shawl around her shoulders and opened the door. "I'd better take Joshua his supper. It's freezing out in the fields tonight."

"Give him my regards," said the baker woman.

Her cat stretched. The fire in the oven cracked and a warm glow spread all over the house. The baker woman went on kneading the bread. Flomp, thump, thump, she went, as she slapped the dough and pummelled it with her fist.

"All this work just for a flat piece of bread," she thought, rolling out the dough until it covered the table.

Suddenly there was a knock at the door.

"Hello!" a voice called.

"There's no more bread until tomorrow," cried the baker woman.

"We don't want bread," replied the voice.

"Come in, then," said the baker woman.

The door opened, and a young man in a blue robe looked in. His cheeks were red from running and there was a glint of fear in his eyes.

"Can we come in for a while?" he said breathlessly. "The soldiers are after us."

"Soldiers?" said the baker woman.

"King Herod's men," said the young man. "They want to kill our baby."

The baker woman stifled a gasp. "You'd better come in then, quick."

The young man turned and whispered to someone outside. A moment later, a woman stepped inside the bakery. She had a baby in her arms, wrapped in swaddling clothes.

"My name is Mary," she said, "and this is my husband Joseph. Our baby is called Jesus."

"You're all welcome," said the baker woman, bolting the door. "Sit down. You look tired. There's cold milk in the pitcher and some food left over from supper."

"We don't want to be any trouble," Joseph said.

Mary settled down close to the warm oven. "They nearly found us," she whispered, hugging the baby to her breast. "Some of them were waiting behind a rock when we came down the old Egypt road. They shouted to us to stop, but we gave them the slip."

"Don't worry. You're safe here," said the baker woman. "No one ever comes here except children buying bread for their families." She peeled the dough off the table and put it in a large basin, folding it over and over like a sheet. "I'll heat up the milk now, if you'd like some…"

Her words were interrupted by a loud banging at the door.

"Open up, in the name of Herod!" shouted a loud voice.

Joseph and Mary jumped up.

"Just a minute," cried the baker woman. "My hands are covered with dough."

She turned to Mary. "Give me the baby, quick!"

"What are you going to do?" asked Mary.

"The baby," said the baker woman. "Pass him here."

She took the sleeping baby and laid him gently in the basin. "There you are, little one," she said, pulling the large folds of dough over him. "No one will ever guess you're in there."

"Open up, woman," the soldiers shouted angrily.

"Coming," said the baker woman. She unbolted the door and stepped back to let the soldiers in.

"You're hiding a baby," said the officer. He pointed to Mary and Joseph. "They had a baby. We saw them."

"I can't see a baby," said the baker woman. She smiled at one of the soldiers, who looked like her eldest son. "Can you?"

The soldier glared. "I tell you, there's a baby in here," he said.

"Why don't you find him, then?" suggested the baker woman. "But hurry up – I have work to do."

The soldiers started searching the house. They opened cupboards, they drew the shutters, they even poked their spears in the pile of firewood by the oven.

"Found anything yet?" said the baker woman. "Why don't you have a look upstairs?"

"We will," barked the officer. He snapped his fingers and two of the soldiers ran upstairs. Mary, Joseph and the baker woman could hear them marching around, opening chests and looking in wardrobes.

"Nothing, sir," said the one who looked like the baker woman's son, coming downstairs.

The officer grunted. "False alarm," he snapped. "Search the house next door." His men trooped out of the bakery.

"You haven't looked in my basin," the baker woman said cheekily. "I could be hiding a baby in the bread."

"Don't waste my time with your stupid jokes," barked the officer. He left without another word, scowling.

Joseph shut the door behind him. "That was close," he said.

"My heart nearly stopped," Mary whispered. She unfolded the dough and picked up her baby.

"The poor mite's covered in flour," said the baker woman.

Then she looked at the basin and her mouth fell open. "Look, the dough is rising!" she cried.

It was true. The flat dough was growing bigger and bigger, filling the basin and overflowing on to the table.

"Now I have enough dough to make bread for everyone in the street!" cried the baker woman. She started pulling bits of dough from the basin and rolling them into small loaves.

"Thank you," she said. "Thank you so much. You are going to make a lot of people happy tomorrow."

"You've earned your good fortune," Joseph said. He opened the door and led Mary out. "Goodbye, baker woman, and thank you."

"Goodbye," said the old woman. She stood watching her visitors walk away down the road. Then she went back indoors and started baking. Soon she had made enough bread for everyone in the village.

Ever since then, bakers all over the world have put their dough aside for a while, so that it will rise and grow bigger. That way, they can make more bread to feed the hungry people in the world.

# Flowers *for* Jesus

## A STORY FROM MEXICO

ANNA and her Papa sat huddled together, nibbling bread and bits of goat's cheese.

"Are you warm enough under that blanket?" Papa asked the little girl. "It's cold tonight."

"I'm fine," said Anna. She looked at the herd grazing on the hill around them. "How many goats have we got now, Papa?" she asked.

"Twelve," replied Papa. "We'll have fifteen soon. Then we can buy you some nice clothes, little one. And some sandals, too. I hate seeing you walk around barefoot. It's not very ladylike."

"I'm not a lady," giggled Anna. "I'm a goatherd, Papa."

"I wish you could be something better than a goatherd," said Papa.

"But I like looking after goats," said Anna. "It's what our people have always done."

"I know," said Papa. "Now lie down and get some sleep, little one. It's well past your bedtime."

Anna lay back under her blanket and looked up at the stars. There were so many of them! The moon smiled at her through the branches of a fig tree. It was huge and bright, like an innkeeper's lamp. Anna listened to the shepherds singing lullabies to their children. Then she closed her eyes and drifted off to sleep.

The next thing she knew, Papa was shaking her awake.

"Little one, look at the sky."

Anna opened her eyes. Big, low clouds were filling the heavens, blotting out the moon and stars. They were not ordinary clouds: they seemed to be made of gold and light; their insides glowed like coals on a dying fire, and their edges shimmered.

"They're wonderful!" Anna cried, and she stood up to see them better.

All at once the clouds parted, like curtains before a stage. Hundreds of angels appeared, their silver wings glittering in a bright light that seemed to shine out of their faces.

"Don't be afraid," said the angels. "We bring you tidings of great joy, for a Saviour is born today who is Christ the Lord."

One of them looked straight at Anna and her father. "This shall be a sign to you," he said. "You will find the baby wrapped in swaddling clothes and lying in a manger."

The sky darkened once more, and the angels disappeared. The stars returned, blinking weakly in the firmament.

Anna and her father stood rooted to the spot, unable to move or speak. All around them, shepherds and goatherds were gathering up their crooks and bundles. Children shouted to their sheep, whistling loudly.

"We must go and see the newborn Saviour," said one of the shepherds, a stout fellow with a big beard. "We must be the first to see him."

"But where is he?" asked an old goatherd, wrapping his wine bottle in a napkin. "Where shall we find him?"

The shepherd with the big beard turned and pointed to a bright star hovering above an old barn on a hill nearby. "He is there," he said. "Follow me, everyone."

From all over the hillside, shepherds and goatherds started walking towards the barn. Anna looked at her father. "Shall we go too?" she asked.

"Of course, little one," he said. "We have been waiting for the Saviour for a long time."

He picked up his old crook and the wicker basket that held the rest of their food. Anna whistled to the goats and they came running across the short grass, mewling and bleating.

"Come on," Anna said to them. "We're off to see the Saviour."

They hurried down the hill and along a narrow, twisting path. Shepherds passed them by, eager to see the new baby. The star grew bigger and brighter as they drew near the barn, until they realised it wasn't a star at all, but an enormous lamp hung above the doorway.

Anna could see people inside, kneeling around a manger. A cow and a donkey stood behind, the cow breathing noisily. The Saviour's mother was sitting next to the donkey. She looked drawn and tired, but her eyes shone with a peaceful light.

"I've brought the Saviour a blanket," said one of the shepherds. "It's nice and thick, so it'll keep him warm through the winter months."

"Thank you," said the Saviour's father. He put the blanket over the baby, tucking it around the infant's feet.

"I've brought him a pair of doves," said a shepherd, who had slipped past Anna into the barn. "They'll make nice pets when he's a little older."

"You are most kind," said the Saviour's mother.

The shepherd put the dove's cage down beside all the other presents at the foot of the manger: a jar of figs, a keg of oil, a little wooden cart, some eggs in a basket.

"We have brought nothing for the baby," said Anna. "Papa, shall I go home and fetch one of our rabbits, or a mat?"

"Alas, there is nothing to fetch," said her father. "Your mother has just sold the last of the rabbits, and the landlord has taken our mats instead of rent."

"But we can't go into the barn without a present," cried Anna. "It would seem rude."

"We'll just have to look at the Saviour from out here," Papa said.

"I want to see him properly," said Anna sadly. She looked around in the hope of finding something to give the baby – some berries, perhaps, or a bunch of wild flowers.

"Never mind, Anna," Papa said. "We can pay our respects just as well from here."

"But I want to touch the baby," Anna cried. "And I must find him a present!"

She ran into the dark meadow. What could she give? There were only weeds. "I'll take him a bunch of weeds," said Anna. "It's better than nothing."

She started picking the prettiest weeds she could find, taking care not to break the tender stalks.

Behind her, a dog barked.

Anna turned and saw an angel in the sky above her, his silver wings shining in the moonlight.

"Have you nothing to bring the Saviour?" the angel asked.

"No," answered Anna, "nothing but these weeds." She held out the green leaves for the angel to see.

"But they are so pretty," said the angel kindly. He reached out and a bright spark passed from his fingers to the weeds. The green leaves turned a bright scarlet, the colour of a king's robe.

"There," said the angel. "Now you can give the Saviour a very special gift." He spread his wings, and a moment later he was gone.

"Anna," Papa said, coming into the meadow. "Who was that you were talking to?"

Anna was too dumbfounded to speak. She held out the flowers for her father to see.

"I have never seen such flowers," said Papa. "Where did you get them, little one?"

"An angel gave them to me," Anna whispered.

She hurried into the barn and laid her flowers at the baby's feet.

"How beautiful!" said the baby's mother. "What are they called, little girl?"

"They have no name," said Anna. "They are still new."

"Then we shall call them Christmas flowers," said the baby's mother, picking up the sleeping baby and placing him gently in Anna's arms, "in celebration of my son's birth."

"Now what can I do?" Kumbi wondered. "I can't go to Granny's empty-handed." She walked across the cracked river-bed, thinking.

"I know," she said. "I'll go and ask the plantation workers."

She ran to the sugar plantation. "Have you any water to spare?" she asked the workers.

"Not a drop," they replied.

Kumbi thanked them all the same. Then she went to see her friends the chicken farmers. "Have you any water to spare?" she asked.

"None at all," said the farmers sadly.

"Never mind," said Kumbi, trying to sound cheerful. "The rains will come soon. Have a nice Christmas." She turned away from the farm and kept on walking. She was hungry and thirsty, but she didn't dare stop. She just had to find some water for Granny.

"Have you any water to spare?" she asked everyone she met. No one had.

The sun began to set, and Kumbi was about to give up. Then she remembered Princess Abeena. By now, her servants might have brought water from the city.

Kumbi hurried across the fields towards Abeena's village.

She found the princess sitting in a drum of water.

"Please, Your Highness," she asked, "may I have some water for my granny?"

"Certainly not," snapped the princess. "My father paid good money for this water."

"But you're wasting it," cried Kumbi, "while other people are nearly dying of thirst."

"That's no concern of mine," replied the princess, "Now get out of my sight, or I shall ask my father's men to throw you out."

Kumbi picked up her gourd and ran back into the bush.

It was getting late. The evening star was twinkling in the sky.

"It's not fair," Kumbi cried. "It's just not fair."

Across the fields she could hear the church bells calling everyone to the carol service. Kumbi was too tired to walk any more. Her mum and sisters would have to go to church without her.

She sat down on a stone. A bird flew across the sky. A pale moon came out. More stars joined the evening star, glinting like diamonds.

"What can I do?" thought Kumbi. "I've asked everyone I know for water."

"Kumbi," whispered a voice from the bushes. "You haven't asked me."

Startled, Kumbi looked around her. "Who said that?" she said.

"I have water, Kumbi."

"Who are you?" Kumbi cried. "Where are you?"

"I am all around you, Kumbi."

In the church across the fields, the choir started singing.

> *Jesus Saviour is born!*
> *Our Lord and Saviour is born,*
> *Goodwill to men, Jesus Saviour is born.*

"I am born," whispered the voice.

"Are you the Christ-child?" asked Kumbi, looking up.

"I was thirsty once," went on the voice, "and someone gave me water to drink."

"I'm thirsty too," said Kumbi.

There was a bright flash, and a cluster of stars seemed to fall from the sky.

Kumbi looked at the gourd. It was full of water!

"Thank you," Kumbi said. "Thank you very much, Christ-child." She lifted the gourd to her lips and drank deeply. Then she put the gourd on her head and hurried towards Granny's.

On the way, she met some men coming home from work on their donkeys. "Where did you get that water?" they asked.

"I asked the Christ-child for it," Kumbi said.

"Give us some, please," the workers begged. Kumbi let them drink. When they'd finished, she looked into the gourd. It was still full!

"It's a miracle," said one of the farm hands.

"Yes," Kumbi said, "a miracle."

She hurried on to Granny's village. The villagers were streaming out of the carol service.

"Please give us some water," they said, when they saw Kumbi's gourd.

Kumbi poured water into their cupped hands. Other people came running with jugs and calabashes. Kumbi filled everyone's pots. And the more she poured, the more water there was in her gourd.

"It's the gourd of plenty!" cried the villagers. "Come and see, everyone!"

The rest of the village came running and shouting. Granny was there among them.

"Have faith in me, Kumbi," whispered the Christ-child's voice in Kumbi's ear, "and I shall answer all your prayers."

# Babushka

## A STORY FROM RUSSIA

BABUSHKA looked out of the window. It was a sunny morning and children were playing out in the snow.

She watched them for a moment, then turned away. She had better things to do than stand looking out of the window. There were cabbages to slice and curtains to mend and the old stove needed polishing. She liked her house to be spick and span and she liked her visitors to wipe their feet on the mat when they came to visit. Not that she had many visitors – her cottage stood outside the village, with only robins and foxes to keep her company through the long, dark winter.

Seeing the children made Babushka feel sad. She reached under her bed and pulled out a wicker basket full of toys. They were all a bit broken because she had bought them second-hand from a market. She had meant to mend them to give to her own child. No need now. The baby had died before he was old enough to play with them.

Tears came to her eyes. She was lonely without her son. Still, not having a child left her a lot of time for cleaning and polishing – hers was the tidiest house in the village.

A sudden shout made Babushka run to the window.

A long line of strange beasts with humps was coming up the road. On each beast sat a man, wrapped against the cold in bright, colourful shawls. The three men riding at the front were dressed in fine clothes and furs. One wore a blue turban, held with a diamond brooch. The other two wore crowns.

One of the men riding with them looked up and saw Babushka peering through the window. He smiled. Shyly, Babushka smiled back.

The camels stopped outside her house. The man who had smiled climbed down and trudged up the garden path. "May we stop here for the night?" he asked, peeling the scarf away from his face. "My masters are tired."

"I have only cabbage soup and bread to offer you," said Babushka, "but you are all welcome to stay."

The stranger turned and called to his companions. His three masters came into the house, followed by their servants.

"My name is Melchior," said the first man, shaking Babushka's hand. "I am a king and an astronomer."

"And I am Caspar," said the second man.

"They call me Balthasar," said the third. "We are following the star."

"The star?" asked Babushka. "What star?"

"The bright star that we believe will lead us to the King," replied Melchior. "He will be born in a stable. His name will be Jesus."

"You talk in riddles," said Babushka. She wished she'd had time to sweep the floor and put away the frying-pan.

"No," said Caspar, "there really is a star. We have been following it for many weeks. It will lead us to the King."

"A king?" Babushka put the soup on the stove and started cutting the bread. "What sort of king?"

"The King of Kings, the Saviour of the world," said Balthasar. "He will rule over this world and the next."

"He is only a baby now," said Melchior.

"A baby," said Babushka, thinking of the toys lying in the wicker basket under the bed. "How nice."

"Why not come along with us to see him, Babushka?" said Melchior. "Then you too can see the great King born in a stable. You seem to be lonely here."

"Maybe I will," said Babushka. She ladled out the soup and put the bread on the table. The three kings and their servants ate hungrily. When they had finished, Babushka put the dishes in the sink.

"We will sleep now until evening," said Melchior. "We don't want to lose track of the star."

The servants spread thick furs on the floor and everyone lay down to sleep – everyone except Babushka. She sat in a chair by the fire and darned socks.

As the sun was setting, the three kings rose and prepared for the journey ahead.

"Come with us, Babushka," said Melchior, as they took their leave. "It is going to be a clear night. I can see our guiding star already."

"I'd love to," Babushka cried. "But I can't leave until I have tidied up the house."

"You can catch up with us later, then," said Caspar. "I'm afraid we can't wait for you. The star might disappear."

Soon the long line of camels had disappeared down the road, their bells tinkling in the freezing air.

Babushka went back indoors. She washed the dishes, put out the rubbish and ironed her clothes. "I must look nice to meet the baby King," she said to herself.

By the time she had finished all her chores she was tired, and she went to bed.

When she awoke next morning, the wind had blown dust into the house. Babushka got out her mop and bucket. "I shall join their three majesties just as soon as I finish," she promised herself.

But time passed, and somehow, she always found another chore to do.

"Weren't you going to follow the kings, Babushka?" asked the people from the village.

"Yes, yes," she said, "but first I must tidy the house."

She knelt down to clean under the bed, and saw the basket full of toys. How nice it would be to give them to someone to play with! She mended the broken toys and put them back in the basket.

Then she locked her cottage door and started off down the road.

"Have you seen three kings going by on camels?" she asked everyone she met.

"We have," they replied. "They went that way."

So Babushka followed the kings' trail across the great plain, on and on, over mountains and across valleys, holding tightly to her basket so that the toys wouldn't fall out.

At long last she reached a big city.

"His Majesty must surely be born by now," she said to herself. She walked through street after street, looking into prams. "Are you the one?" she asked every baby she saw. "Are you the King of Kings?"

None of the babies replied. But children began to crowd round her, wide-eyed and wondering who she was. Babushka opened her basket and started giving out the toys she had brought. The children's eyes sparkled and they laughed with delight.

"Thank you!" they cried.

Babushka wandered over the hill to the next town, and on to the next, handing out tops and bricks and rag-dolls. To her surprise, the basket never ran out. The more toys she gave away, the more seemed to appear.

Some people say she is still wandering from place to place, searching for the King of Kings and handing out presents from her miraculous basket. Perhaps next Christmas she will bring you a gift!

# Author's Note

## The Brave Little Camel

Christian communities in Syria celebrate Christmas right up to Epiphany on January 6th. Children leave out bowls of water and wheat for the brave little camel who brings them presents.
**Source:** Told to me by the late Father Robert Darmanin in Malta. I have added details from *Christmas Customs Around the World*, by H.H.Wernecker (Bailey Brothers and Swinfen, 1974).

## Baby in the Bread

The Maltese love their breads, cakes and pastries. The traditional sweet at Christmas is *qaghaqa tal-ghasel*, a pastry ring stuffed with treacle, jam and candied peel.
**Source:** Told to me by Robert Darmanin. The story comes from a mediaeval pan-European fable, probably based on apocryphal gospels. It is retold in *It's Time for Christmas*, by Elizabeth Hough Sechrist and Janette Woolsey (Macrae Smith, 1959).

## Flowers for Jesus

This is an amalgamation of two well-known stories: *The Christmas Rose*, in which a girl gives the newborn baby Jesus roses provided by an angel; and *The First Poinsettia*, a Mexican fable telling how a girl offers poinsettias, also miraculously provided, on a church altar during midnight mass.
**Source:** Told to me by Ricardo Jimenez, an Argentinian from Tucumán.

## The Gourd of Plenty

In Ghana, on Christmas Eve, Christians light fireworks, then go to church (which is often decorated with a palm tree) for midnight mass and a nativity play. On Christmas Day, children wake up very early and go carol-singing. Christmas dinner is usually goat, chicken or fish accompanied by pounded yam, okra soup and porridge with beans.
**Source:** Based on Ghanaian traditions described in *Christmas Customs Around the World*, by H.H.Wernecker (Bailey Brothers and Swinfen, 1974).

## Babushka

It is not Father Christmas or Santa Claus who brings presents in Russia, but Babushka. In some places, her role is taken by a white-robed lady called Kolyada, who travels in a sleigh. People sing carols to her, and are rewarded with a gift.
**Source:** Retold from *The Christmas Book*, by Esme Eve (Chatto & Windus, 1970), and *The Silver Treasure: Myths and Legends of the World*, by Geraldine McCaughrean (Orion, 1996).